IF

Geoh's Back To School

L.C. Young

ISBN 978-1-63844-411-4 (paperback)
ISBN 978-1-63844-413-8 (hardcover)
ISBN 978-1-63844-412-1 (digital)

Christian Faith Publishing, Inc.
832 Park Avenue
Meadville, PA 16335
www.christianfaithpublishing.com

Printed in the United States of America

MY BELOVED…

My Beloved ~ It's about time! But you and I know that God's time is always the best and perfect time, and though this book has been on our prayer radar for 3 years it's been on the to do list for 25 years! Thank you for being my constant, my steadfast, my encourager, my spiritual partner, my home and for asking me for a ride home that one starry night 35 years ago! Always know I'll love you from now until forever and more…and now everyone knows that too!

To My Children and Grandchildren

You all have added so much love, joy and amazement to my soul! Both collectively and individually more than one mother, mother-in-law, Tutu's heart could possibly hold! Out of my love for you all has been in part of the inspiration of this children's series and I pray that you see that love through the pages. I thank God for each and every one of you daily for being in my life and for being my sunshine's! And always remember to just try! Love you plenty and I miss you more! And always remember any day is a good day to color eggs and have a parade!

DAD & MOM

You once told me at the age of 15 "something in you must believe you are good enough to give yourself the opportunity to just try..." Well, because of that statement it's been one of my motto's ever since and the full inspiration of this children's book series. Because of that mindset its' allowed me to pick myself up, dust myself off when I've fallen and keep on trying. Thank you, mom, for being my first and biggest cheerleader and wanting to witness every detail no matter how great or difficult it was at the time you were always there if you could be there. Encouraging me to hope and dream as big as I wanted to dream and instilling in me to never put a cap on my sky. Now as a parent myself I understand why you would say daily "I love you more than you will ever, ever know." and for that there are no words worthy enough to describe the thankfulness I feel and I will carry my love for you eternally...

Dad, we did it! Like mom there are no words to describe my gratitude for the sacrifice you had given to assure that I knew I was being raised in a home full of love, imperfect like most families but nonetheless I was loved every day. Thank you for helping me be the mother and person that I am today. You were both so committed and intentional with your thoughts and love for me as parents enough to last two lifetimes, that all I can say or do at the least is dedicate this children's book first in its' series to both of you, for if it wasn't for you two and God, I would be nothing. You once told me this old Hawaiian proverb saying:

"If you want to plan for 1 year plant Kalo
If you want to plan for 10 years plant Koa
However, if you want to plan for 100 years, teach the children."

a hui hou ka kou ~

If all my schoolbooks were coloring books and comic books
Oh! What a place this would be…
I'd stay in the lines and dress in my disguise!
And see all the possibilities…

If only all the schoolbooks were coloring books and comic books
Oh, What a place this would be!

If all my toys were here in my classroom,
Oh! What a place this would be!
I'd never be bored or feel ignored...
Oh! All the possibilities!
Oh, What a place this would be!

5

If all the school lunch was everything I did want,
Oh, What a place this would be!
I would eat all I want and never talk at lunch!
Oh! What a place this would be!

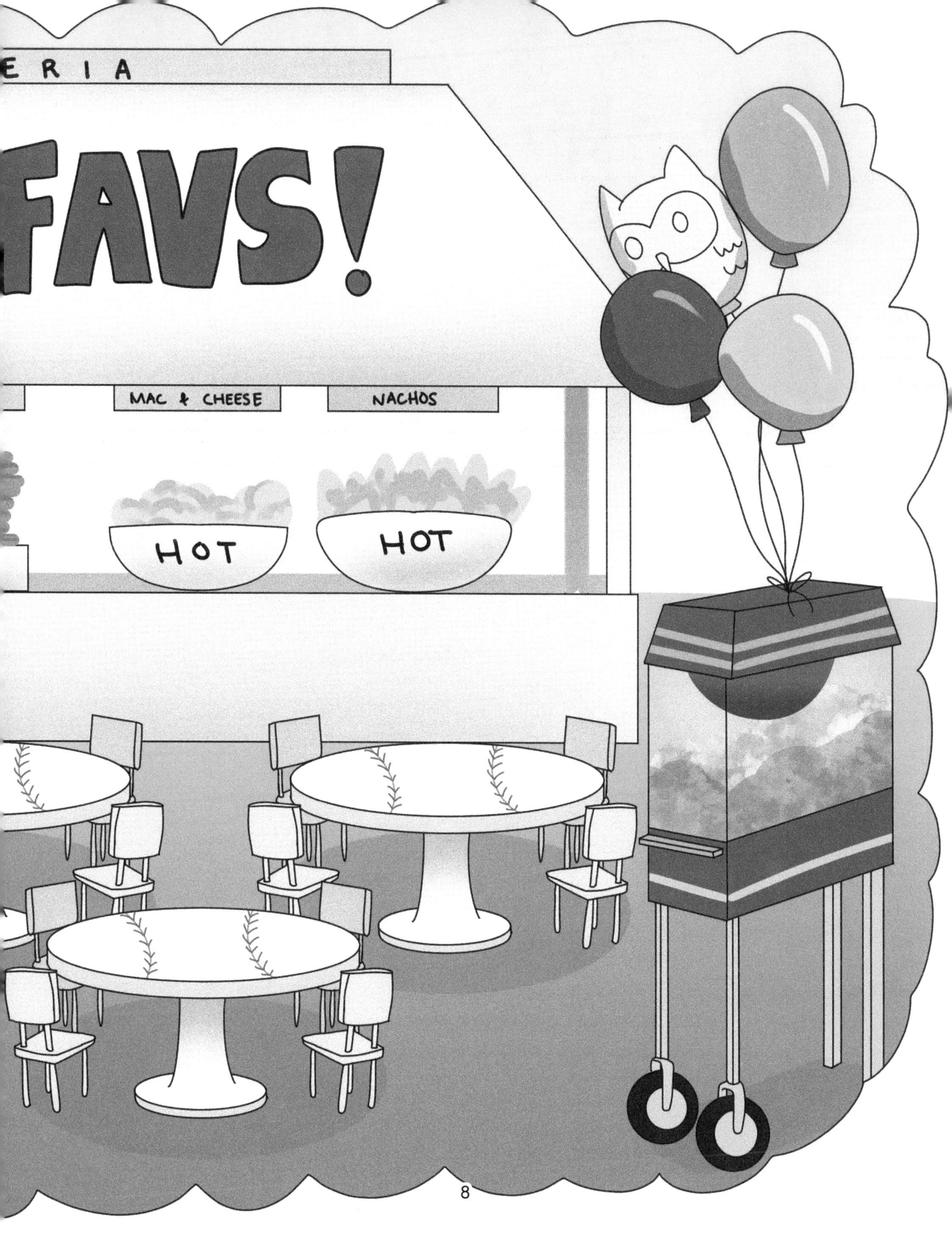
ERIA
FAVS!
MAC & CHEESE
NACHOS
HOT
HOT

If all the whiteboards were skateboards and snowboards
Oh! What a place this would be!
We'd go outside and see where we'd glide!
Oh! What a place this would be!

Then, one day, Mom said just TRY…
If I could see that school is really good for me,
Oh! What a place this would be!
I would see the teacher's helping me to be the best that I can be
All I need to do is just try to give the best of me…
If I could see that school is really good for me
Oh! What a place this could be!
Oh! What a place this could be!

If I could see the friends I could meet…
Oh! What a place this could be!
I might ride the bus and even try some new school lunch!
Oh! What a place this could be!
If I could get myself to see that school is the place to be,
Oh! What a thing that could be!

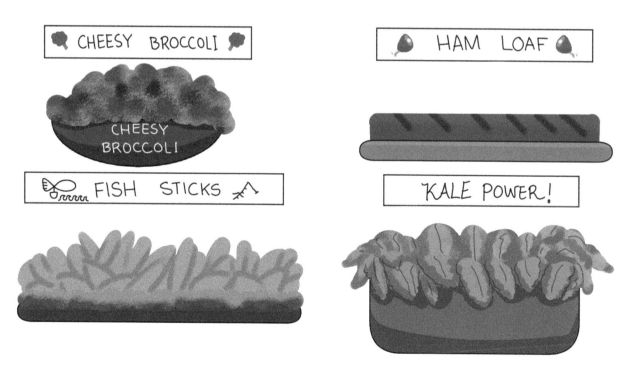

If all my nervousness was nothing but courage
Oh! What a place this could be!
I'd be first in class and never even miss a class!
Oh! What a place this could be!

#1
GEOH
COURAGE A+
BRAVE
FEARLESS
"WHEN I GROW UP"
I want to be
several things
but first I see
myself going to college
and playing Baseball
and basketball forever. I
also want to build my
mom a new house.
WRITTEN BY GEOH

If all my fears were nothing but dreams and hopes,
Oh! What a place this could be!
I'd try to participate and maybe even create!
Oh! What a place this could be!

If I could see that trying things are good things
Oh! What a place this could be!
Changing grades or changing schools or even making new friends
All can be scary even for me!

If I could only see that trying things are good things
Oh! What a place this could be!

If all could see all the possibilities that was created in me to be!

Oh! What a place this could be!

Oh! What a place this could be with a little belief in me!

If given the chance to be what I'm supposed to be
Oh! What a place this could be!

If I had someone telling me I'm someone

who could be anything I could be…

I'd try my best to do my best…

And that is good enough for me…

Oh! What a place this could be!

Oh! What a place this could be!

The Beginning...

The power of words daily can both empower a
person or take away their hopes and dreams…
Therefore, let us focus on building our children
up and helping them reach their full potential in
life and fulfilling their own possibilities of…

"If"

About the Author

L. C. Young is a wife and has been happily married for thirty-five years. She is a mother to three grown children, a "Tutu" (grandmother in the Hawaiian language) to four beautiful granddaughters, one handsome grandson, and loyal companion to three dogs named Suki, Pika, and Christmas! But before all this, she is first the daughter of George and Hatsuko, who were the inspiration of this book series. The main character was named and created using the first initials of her parents' first names as a tribute to them. You see, she knew she was raised by perfectly imperfect parents just as she herself is. Now having raised her children with her husband, she wants to thank them for the perfectly imperfect life that they gave her. Raising her with love and affirmation the best they knew how in a world that sometimes, as we all know, can be not so kind—they gave her the best of themselves every day, showing her through simple and sometimes even quiet moments how to succeed even in adversity.

Dear Lord…

I could not have written this book without you, not one word without clarity. I thank you for putting my thoughts together, for putting the right people in my life and on this path and for guiding me every step of the way. Thank you for shinning the light where it seemed dark and uncertain I knew you were with me, because things became brighter for with you there is no darkness for you are the light. Thank you for quieting the world during a time that the waters surrounding were troubled and I was straining to hear you, but as you silence the calamity and I heard you when I went to you in prayer. Thank you for loving me. Thank you for standing with me. Thank you for never leaving me Thank you for what's to come…

Thank you, amen.

CPSIA information can be obtained
at www.ICGtesting.com
Printed in the USA
LVHW070453191021
700832LV00012B/946